The Strongest Man

By Jesse Orenshein

Illustrated by Madison Lovo

Grandpa Herbie's Stories

Visit
GrandpaHerbiesStories.com
For more rhyming adventure books like this!

A GRANDPA HERBIE'S STORIES BOOK

First Edition 2018
Published in the United States by
Grandpa Herbie's Stories
Los Angeles, CA 90035

Summary: In Ancient Greece, a scrawny schoolboy tricks the neighborhood jock into using his incredible physical strength to make a positive impact on the world.

The Strongest Man

ISBN-13: 978-1724425232
ISBN-10: 1724425234

Give the gift of reading!

_____

_____

_____

_____

Dedicated to my children. Every day,
I try to be stronger for you.

-JO

To my Dad.
Thank you for always being
my biggest cheerleader.

-ML

Brick was the strongest boy in the school.
He loved being strong 'cause it made him feel cool.
He loved being mean to the kids who were weak,
And they didn't talk back. They were too scared to speak.

Larry was the weakest boy in the school.
But he knew that Brick wasn't actually cool.
"A strong person could do lots of good," Larry thought,
"Because someone who's strong can help those who are not."

At graduation, Larry came up with a trick.
A very smart trick to fool that mean Brick.
He said, "Brick, as soon as you walk out that door,
You will not be the strongest boy anymore."

"You're only the strongest because we're at school,
Where the kids are so weak that they can't lift a stool.
But adults in the city are stronger," he said.
"I heard one guy can lift a cow over his head!"

"You can still be the strongest, but it won't be fun,
And you'll have to start now
'Cause there's work to be done."

"Build a great stadium. That's your first mission.
Then challenge the town to a great competition!
Let everyone watch, and then only then,
I'll admit that Great Brick is the strongest again."

Brick was upset, but Larry was right,
So he worked for a year, all day and all night,
On the greatest stadium the city had seen.
And for one year, Brick didn't have time to be mean.

It was just the first summer, but people poured in
Because everyone wanted to see who would win.

Brick ran so fast,
That the air turned to steam,

And he rowed so hard
That he drained a whole stream.

Then he jumped so high
Above the high bar,
That everyone's necks hurt
From turning so far.

The people erupted with laughter and cheers
For the most awesome summer in 800 years.
But Larry was quiet. He let out a sigh.
He wasn't impressed, and then he said why:

"You're the strongest in the city. This much is true,
But every big city has someone like you.
So if you want to beat them and show us your worth,
You'll have to prove you're the strongest on Earth."

Brick was outraged, but Larry was right,
So he worked for two years, all day and all night,

On the greatest stadium the world's ever seen.
And for two years, Brick didn't have time to be mean.

That summer, the games were the biggest affair,
With a crowd crowding in from every-which-where.

Brick leaped over hurdles
Eleven feet high,

And hurled a javelin
Right through the sky.

He shredded across the pool like a shark,
And he still wasn't tired when day turned to dark.

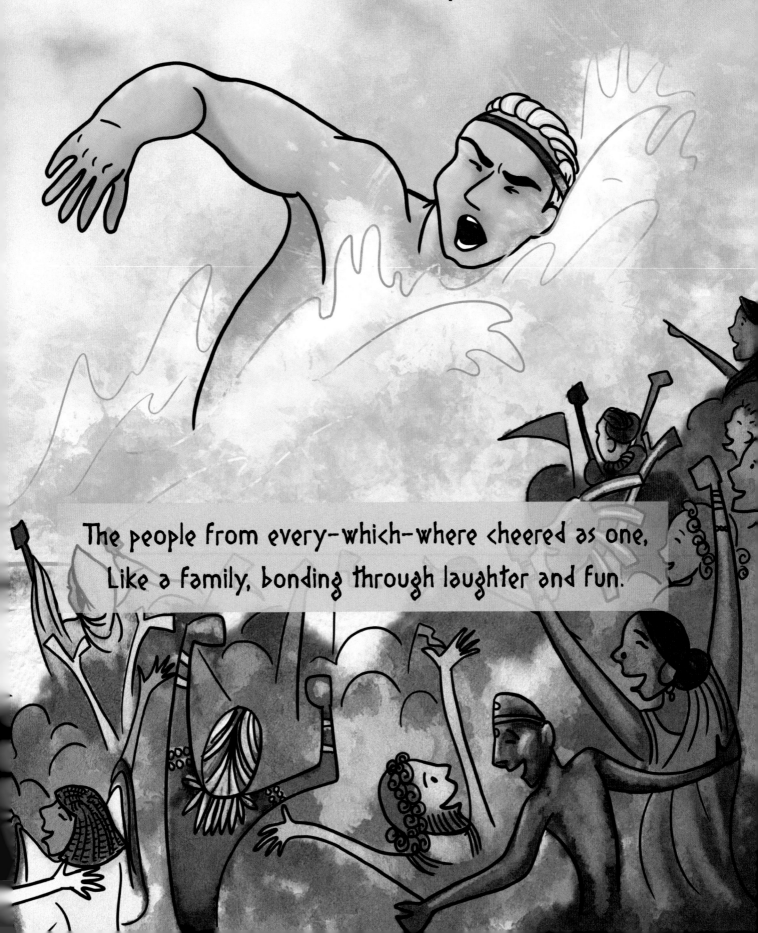

The people from every-which-where cheered as one,
Like a family, bonding through laughter and fun.

But again, little Larry was far from impressed
'Cause not everyone got to see Brick at his best.
"The poor people," he said, "can't afford their own seat
To see how many strong men you defeat."

"This stadium needs to have poor people in it.
Until that day comes, I just won't admit it."

Brick was done building stadiums. Done with these tricks.

He knew this was something that money could fix.

Being the strongest earned Brick lots of gold.

So much, that it took 23 banks to hold.

And the next day, Brick walked

Through the biggest bank's door,

And donated all of his wealth to the poor.

And the next summer...

Brick spelled out his name
With forty-three arrows,

Then lifted 10,000 pounds
And six sparrows.

He climbed up a mountain
And dove from a peak

That was so high that climbing it
Took a whole week.

Finally, Brick had
won his last game.
He was finally done
earning money and fame.

All of the people had
watched him win gold,
From the poor and the rich
to the young and the old.

Even dogs and cats
were part of the buzz.
At last the world knew
who the strongest man was.

But even though Brick was the strongest of all,
One day, the big champion took a big fall.
He injured himself from his toe to his head,
So the doctor told him to stay in his bed,

And as we all know, if you don't exercise,
Then your muscles will shrink to a much smaller size.
So when Larry came by, Brick struggled to speak.
"Are you happy now, Larry? I'm weaker than weak."

Larry chuckled and giggled, then laughed till he cried,
"Silly, Brick! True strength is on the inside!
You're not the strongest for running or rowing
Or jumping or swimming or javelin throwing.
You're strong 'cause you used everything that you've got
To make the world better when others could not."

"Just look at all of the people who traded
Their frowning for smiles at the games you created.
Everyone's happy now. Everyone's friends.
The cities are booming. The fun never ends."

"The poor and the rich
Are no longer apart.
We all live together,
And that's just the start.
You've taught us that everyone's
Strong in some way,
And new people are finding
Their strength every day."

Brick apologized to Larry for being a bully.
He thanked him truly, completely, and fully.
Larry hugged the champion who used to be mean,
And began the strongest friendship the world's ever seen.

THE END

(But keep reading) →

Story Questions

1. Who do you think is stronger: Brick, or Larry?
2. Is it possible to be strong without looking strong on the outside?
3. What makes you strong?
4. How can you use your strength to make the world better?
5. What big competition do we have today, that brings the whole world together?
6. What can we learn from Larry and the way he handled Brick's bullying?
7. Brick didn't realize that he was doing a good thing for the world. Do you think it counts if someone does something good without realizing it?
8. Can you think of someone in your life who does good things without expecting a medal, or anything else in return? (Perhaps the person reading you this story...)

www.GrandpaHerbiesStories.com

Family Olympics

1. Come up with your own Olympic sports, using ONLY things that you already have in the house.

2. Take turns competing in each sport, and record your results on the provided charts. (See example below.)

3. Cut out the medals on the last page, and present them to the winners (ideally at a huge ceremony in front of the whole town).

Example:

Couch Diving

Rules: Each athlete takes a running start and dives onto the couch, completing a trick in mid-air before landing. Tricks are rated on a scale of 1-10 by a panel of unbiased judges.

Athlete	Description	Score
Mom	Quadruple backflip	8
Dad	Belly flop karate chop	2
Uncle Joe	Corkscrew gainer	5
Jamie	The flaming lion	$7\frac{1}{2}$
Alex	Somersault pole vault	6
Baby Sam	There is no way to describe this trick	10

Athlete		Score

Athlete		Score

Athlete		Score

Athlete		Score

Athlete		Score

Athlete		Score

And the
winner is...

Made in the USA
Monee, IL
05 July 2024

61291234R00026